The Yearbook

The Yearbook

A Time-Travel Love Story

PAUL H. SCHNEITER

LitPrime Solutions
21250 Hawthorne Blvd
Suite 500, Torrance, CA 90503
www.litprime.com
Phone: 1 (209) 788-3500

This is a work of fiction. All of the characters, names, incidents, organizations, and dialogue in this novel are the products of the author's imagination or are used fictitiously.

Published by LitPrime Solutions   03/05/2021

ISBN: 978-1-953397-43-0(sc)
ISBN: 978-1-953397-44-7(hc)
ISBN: 978-1-953397-45-4(e)

Library of Congress Control Number: 2020923569

Contents

Dedication

For those blessed to believe that which is unbelievable.

Preface

The concept of traveling into the past and into the future has fascinated humankind for centuries. The ancients fantasized about moving forward in time. There is, for example, the Japanese tale of a young fisherman who journeys to a palace under the sea. When he returns home after three days, he discovers he has advanced 300 years into the future.[1] In a Jewish legend, a 1st-century BC scholar falls asleep for seventy years. When he awakens, all the people he knew are gone.

Among the earliest accounts of backward time travel are French botanist Pierre Boitard's 1861 book *Paris Before Men,* and Edward E. Hale's book *Hands Off,* also published in 1861. Then, of course, there is Charles Dickens' classic, *A Christmas Carol* (1843), which includes an account of time travel in both directions.

The idea of time travel by machine likely began with Edward Page Mitchell's *The Clock That Went Backward* (1881), published in the *New York Sun*. But it was H.G. Wells' *The Time Machine* (1895) that gave currency to the concept of mechanically driven time travel.

Many scientists believe backward time travel isn't likely to happen. That fact notwithstanding, the concept has inspired countless articles, books, television shows, and motion pictures, including this book. Its plot, if not unique, is novel. A young woman falls in love with a young

---

[1] Source: "History of the time travel concept." <u>Wikipedia</u>. Source is the same for the other facts cited herein.

man whose photograph she sees in a 1937 university yearbook. She becomes obsessed with him and devotes herself to finding a way to travel through time to meet him. Eventually, she succeeds. Thus, *The Yearbook* is more than a time-travel story; it is, I suggest, an intriguing, captivating love story.

I express heartfelt appreciation to my wife, Pat, for conceptualizing the plot and for her exemplary support. I express appreciation as well to my publisher whose staff went the extra mile time and again on my behalf.

1

How It Began

Elizabeth tried to hide her excitement from the other passengers as the Greyhound neared Logandale where she would be living and going to school. She had been seeing an increasing number of farmhouses, barns, and cattle behind barbed wire and white fences.

It had been a long ride from her city in the mid-west, during which she thought about her loving mother, controlling father, and baseball-crazy little brother. She smiled as she recalled how her father told her she had enough education for a woman. It was that attitude, and others like it, that got Elizabeth interested in the women's rights movement and turned her to sociology as a major.

The sound of the Greyhound's air brakes caused Elizabeth to unfasten her seat belt and prepare to exit the bus. It was late afternoon.

Logandale was a farming community with 17,000 residents (20,000 when students were in town). It was set in a pristine valley that turned to scarlet, yellow, and purple with fall's first frosty bite. It smelled of leather and wet wood and newly cut hay.

Blonde, blue-eyed, posture-perfect twenty-year-old Elizabeth was a model of head-turning young womanhood. Her flawless complexion radiated a golden glow. Her figure had melted many male hearts. And her warm, friendly personality enabled her to make friends easily. She had a lot going for her.

Elizabeth had completed two years of junior college. Her 3.9 GPA earned her a full-ride scholarship to Stanton University. It was fall, 2010. A new school year would begin in a matter of days.

The Greyhound turned into the depot and came to a stop.

The sun-glassed driver exited the bus and opened the luggage compartment. Elizabeth picked up her suitcases and watched for Mrs. Ravencroft, the owner of the Stanton Apartments where Elizabeth would live. In minutes, a tall, thin woman in her seventies was walking toward her. She was wearing gold-rimmed glasses, had grey hair, and, by pre-arrangement, displayed a red hat.

"You must be Elizabeth," Mrs. Ravencroft said as she shook Elizabeth's hand. "And, of course, I'm Bella Ravencroft. Please call me by my last name out of respect for my deceased husband, OK?"

"That will be fine," Elizabeth said.

"Welcome to Logandale, home of Stanton University," Mrs. Ravencroft said, adding, "It's wonderful to meet you."

"Such a nice welcome. Thank you," Elizabeth responded. "I'm very happy to be here."

Elizabeth's initial impression of Mrs. Ravencroft was that there was something mysterious about her, something hidden. Part of it was her eerie, high-pitched voice, and part was her close-to-crooked smile.

"Well then, let's get you to your apartment. It's only a five-minute walk. I don't drive anymore. Oh, you look lovely in that plaid skirt and white blouse."

"Thank you," Elizabeth said.

Mrs. Ravencroft took one of the suitcases, and Elizabeth picked up the remaining two.

They had gone only a few steps when a middle-aged man approached Elizabeth.

"Let me help you with those suitcases," he said.

"Oh, no thanks. I'll be fine, not far to go."

Moments passed. "He probably thought I was just another weak woman," Elizabeth half-muttered to Mrs. Ravencroft, who didn't respond.

Stanton University, founded in 1888, was named after William Bennington Stanton, who had helped develop a process that facilitated the home canning of food. He used his wealth to support a variety of life-lifting causes, especially education.

The Stanton Apartment house was an old, two-storey, red-brick structure. Three units were at ground level, with the other three above them. Mrs. Ravencroft occupied the middle ground-floor unit. The two-storey units were fronted by a narrow, wrought-iron walkway that ran the width of the building. They were reached by a single flight of stairs.

"You'll be in the apartment above mine, 2B," Mrs. Ravencroft said, as they climbed the stairs. "It isn't fancy, but you'll be comfortable." She gave Elizabeth what wanted to be a smile.

Elizabeth tried not to show disappointment as they entered the apartment. The living room was small, sparsely furnished, and had a musty smell.

"It will go away now that you're here," Mrs. Ravencroft said, as if reading Elizabeth's mind. "It just needs to be aired out. I should have opened the windows for you this morning."

The kitchen was adequate, equipped with a range, refrigerator, and sink. The bedroom was, however, a pleasant surprise. It was large, with ample closet space, a large bed, and elegant drapes.

"That's about it," Mrs. Ravencroft said. "As you probably know, all financial matters—rent, utilities, books, whatever—have been taken care of. Tell me if there's anything you need."

"Who is paying for everything? I know how scholarships work, but I seem to have received an extra generous one."

"Don't worry about that, dear. Just make the most of it. And be sure to let me know if I can be helpful."

Then, as an afterthought, she added, "The unit to the right is vacant. . . has been for several years. I use it as a storage room, a place for items tenants have left behind. Here are two keys, one for this apartment and one for the vacant unit. Feel free to go in and look around."

Elizabeth took the keys and thanked her landlady.

And then Mrs. Ravencroft was gone, and Elizabeth was alone to contemplate all she had to do to get ready for school. She contemplated something else as well: Why did her scholarship stipulate Stanton University? Was something extraordinary going to happen to her at Stanton?

She suddenly felt tired, so she sprawled on the bed and was soon in a deep sleep.

2

Discovery

For the fall semester, Elizabeth enrolled in four classes designed for junior students: English, sociology, history, and algebra. She quickly grew to love Stanton. The professors were not only knowledgeable and approachable, but they were also excellent teachers. Moreover, she readily made friends among the school's three-thousand-member student body.

One afternoon, after Elizabeth had taken care of her most urgent business, including not only registering but also buying books and getting a student ID card and locker, she decided to look inside the next-door unit. She took a deep breath, approached the door, and turned the key. The door protested as she pushed it forward. It was, indeed, a storage area. Two pairs of skis, a tennis racket, a guitar, shoes, clothing, two Cracker Jack boxes, and soda pop bottles were scattered across the floor. There was a book of Emily Dickinson's poems, a two-volume set of the works of Ralph Waldo Emerson, a newspaper with an article about the planned construction of the *SS Queen Mary*, a set of Callaway golf irons, several Baby Ruth candy bar wrappers, and a stack of *Stanton Today* student newspapers. Almost all of the items were old and from various time periods. The room had the same musty smell Elizabeth encountered on her first visit to the apartment.

As she was about to leave, Elizabeth noticed something else. It was a yearbook entitled *The Year That Was: Stanton University, 1937*. She picked it up, brushed off the dust, and began thumbing through its yellowed, slightly wrinkled pages. A feeling of sadness overcame her as she looked at the young faces. *They had their hopes,* she thought. *They had their dreams. A handful might have realized them, a mere fraction of a fraction. Now all sleep dreamlessly.*

Elizabeth started to put the book down but turned one more page. It displayed a black-and-white photograph of a young man. Her eyes, by some mysterious force, seemed to be pulled to it. He was impeccably dressed and groomed, movie-star handsome, and seated on the corner of a table. He held a roll of papers in one hand. Elizabeth stared at the photograph, and as she did, a warm feeling suffused her entire body. She was transfixed. The photograph seemed to exert a force that pulled her to within inches of it. There was something almost magnetic about it. The young man seemed to radiate a sense of command, of supreme self-confidence. He appeared to be looking from decades past, right into Elizabeth's very being. His eyes riveted hers, and her heart palpitated. Finally, after long minutes—her body still permeated by warmth—she noted his name was Ryan Richardson. She bent a corner of the page, closed the book, and put it down. The warm feeling immediately left her and was replaced by a case of chills. She was shaking as she left the room and locked the door.

3

Obsession

Elizabeth had an inquiring mind. She was determined to excel as a student and in her career in sociology. Consequently, she immersed herself in classwork. Even as she did, she could not put the yearbook photograph of Ryan Richardson out of her mind. The harder she tried to forget him, the more obsessed she became with him.

Elizabeth wondered what there was about Ryan that so enraptured her. Yes, he was handsome, but she had dated other young men who were handsome. Was it the way he was sitting? That didn't seem to be the explanation. Was it his facial expression, which seemed to be flirting with a smile? Probably not. Elizabeth decided there was no clear-cut answer.

There were moments when she felt he was following her as she walked through the campus. A wave of the warm feeling swept over her in those moments. Her rational, thoughtful approach to events prompted her to rebel at the idea that something supernatural was happening to her. Yet she could not dismiss her feelings as a product of her imagination.

Elizabeth's obsession with Ryan grew. Despite efforts to reason with herself, she began to wonder if there were any way to go back—back in time—to meet Ryan. Although she chided herself for entertaining that idea, she couldn't dismiss it. She checked books out of the University library, including *The Time Machine*, the 1895 classic by H. G. Wells.

She also read *Outlander,* by Diana Gabal; *A Wrinkle in Time,* by Madeleine W'Engle; *Timeline,* by Michael Crichton; and *The End of Eternity,* by Isaac Asimov. But her research didn't end there.

She studied Albert Einstein's time theories, as well as articles in scientific journals about the speed of light and its relationship to time.

Elizabeth did more than read and study about time travel. She experimented with the process. She closed her eyes, held her arms out in front of her, and imagined she was warm and being lifted. She pretended she was floating. She knew such efforts were silly, but doing them made her feel better, gave her hope.

The obsession with Ryan took over her life. One night, unable to sleep, she went to the storage room, opened the yearbook, and stared at the photograph. In her apartment below, Mrs. Ravencroft heard her, quietly climbed the stairs, and silently watched her from the storage room doorway. Finally, she spoke, startling Elizabeth.

"Excuse me. You're up so late. Is there something I can help—why are you looking at that picture of the young man?" she asked assertively.

Elizabeth blushed. "I need to tell you something. I'm attracted to him, mesmerized by him."

"He was at Stanton years before you were even born," Mrs. Ravencroft said, an edge to her voice. "My mother, who was at Stanton the same time as him, told me she had a crush on him. They dated. She also liked a young man named Harold Olsen. I was surprised my mother would confide in me like that, share something so personal."

"Did she tell you anything about him or Harold Olsen?"

"She said Ryan was from an influential family—had money. You can see in the picture he is well-dressed. His parents were killed in a car accident when he was seven. He was raised by his aunt and uncle. They were well-educated people, intellectuals. Harold Olsen was his friend. He was very outgoing, loved to be the center of attention. Also, he was charismatic.

Elizabeth felt Mrs. Ravencroft knew more than she was disclosing, so she pressed her.

"Is there anything else you can tell me?"

"I think my mother said he was very popular and was an officer in student government. In those days, student body leaders had their offices in the Student Union Building (SUB), which, by the way, is going to be torn down."

"Where do you think the picture might have been taken, Mrs. Ravencroft?"

Elizabeth resisted the urge to call the elderly woman Bella even though she didn't like the name Ravencroft. She intended to keep the promise she made at the Greyhound Depot not to call her Bella.

"Oh, yes, you asked where I thought the picture was taken. I don't know, but my guess is that it was taken in the SUB where he had his office."

"The building that's going to be torn down?"

"Yes," Mrs. Ravencroft answered. She put her hands on Elizabeth's shoulders and said, "I have the impression you're thinking of somehow going back in time, even though you haven't said so. You know, going back in time; it's never been done, even though my late husband said 'Believing is halfway to achieving'. I think that has a certain romantic appeal."

"It does seem like a crazy, romantic dream, but I believe what my college science teacher told the class. He said, 'Nothing is impossible; you must suspend disbelief'."

Mrs. Ravencroft patted Elizabeth on the back and excused herself. Elizabeth returned to her room, carrying the book. She slept fitfully, convinced she had to travel through time to 1936 to meet Ryan Richardson.

4

Flight

In the morning, Elizabeth repeatedly told herself what she had told herself all night—that she must try everything in an effort to find Ryan Richardson. She refused to tell herself that he had to be dead. She feared her scholarship was in jeopardy because of her obsession with Ryan.

She reviewed what Mrs. Ravencroft told her, including the fact that Ryan was in student government, and that student body leaders had their offices in the SUB. Elizabeth reasoned that Ryan may have left something—a book with his name in it, or an essay he had written, or *something*.

A few days later, as soon as her last class for the day was over, Elizabeth went to the SUB. The door was unlocked to give access to the men who were preparing the building for demolition. Inside, a room cluttered with desks, chairs, and tables greeted her. She thought it must have been a reception area. It opened to several smaller rooms. "Offices," Elizabeth said to herself. The rooms were empty except for one, which had a desk in it. With her heart pounding, she opened the desk drawer. It was stuffed with papers, including a math study guide with "R. Richardson" written on it. She was about to close the drawer when she saw an envelope taped to the back of it. "Elizabeth" was scrawled across it. Breathlessly, she withdrew it, opened it, and found two rough-edged tickets to the 1936 Stanton Snowball Dance. They had been torn in half but were taped back together.

As Elizabeth held the tickets, the warm, floating feeling she knew well overcame her. For a moment, she seemed to be outside herself.

What she knew next was that she was walking on the Stanton campus, a place she knew well, although the buildings looked newer and the trees smaller.

She was stunned. She had, indeed, gone back in time. She sensed it was 1936 because of the clothes women were wearing and their hairstyles, which she had seen in photos in the yearbook. That feeling was confirmed when she turned a corner by the Stanton Administration Building and saw Ryan. He looked like he did in the photograph.

He was talking with a girl by an elm tree. Elizabeth was immediately jealous of the girl. She felt an odd feeling in her chest. The girl was tall and beautiful. She had a figure that made other women look frumpy. Later, Elizabeth learned the girl's name was Monica, and that she and Ryan had been dating for several weeks. Elizabeth vowed to take the girl's place.

For the moment, however, there was the matter of where she would stay, though she realized she could be taken back to the future at any moment. If that happened right away, she wouldn't need housing in Logandale. She put that thought aside and went to the Administration Building, where she found the housing office.

"My name is Elizabeth—"

"Yes, I know," a smiling, middle-aged female receptionist said.

"We've been expecting you."

"But how—"

"Everything has been arranged. You'll be in the Stanton Dorm, Room 122. Here are the keys. Be sure to read dorm rules. They're posted inside, on the door. Then, lowering her voice, the receptionist added, "Watch out for Stanton boys—they're, ah, frisky."

Elizabeth was amazed that everything had been arranged for her, though mindful of the immensely greater happening of going back in time. She found herself thinking an unseen power was in play.

"Isn't anything impossible?" she asked under her breath.

In the days that followed, Elizabeth was constantly on the lookout for Ryan. She even skipped classes to look for him, putting her scholarship in ever-greater jeopardy. She saw him once, but he was with friends. She knew she must not intrude. On a mellow, falling-leaves afternoon, after a trip to the bookstore, she went to the library to catch up on required reading for her history class. She retrieved two books, sat down at a table, and opened one. She had read only to the third page when she heard a voice.

"You must be taking History 101—you're reading Muzzey's American history book."

Elizabeth was startled. She looked up and was even more startled to discover the speaker was Ryan! She had prepared for this moment, carefully formulating what she would say in approaching Ryan. But he had approached her first, causing her mind to race to find the right response.

"Ah, oh … yes, history. You must have already taken it last semester, huh?" As she spoke, Elizabeth's thoughts strayed to Ryan's lagoon-blue eyes, which she was seeing up close for the first time. Something ran up and down her spine.

"Yes, and I found it quite interesting. Oh, by the way, I'm Ryan Richardson. I couldn't help but notice you—a beautiful girl sitting alone at this table."

Elizabeth blushed.

"You make me feel … I feel special to have you notice me."

"I couldn't help but notice you, a beautiful girl sitting by herself in this stuffy old library."

Elizabeth knew the moment had come when she had to be brave and bold. But she was conflicted. She knew she ran the risk of turning Ryan off. Surely, many girls had "come on" to him. She might appear to be just another such girl, one Ryan could easily dismiss. But when would she have another such opportunity? She decided to press ahead.

"I have seen you with another girl. So, it may be especially inappropriate for me to ask you something. Don't think badly of me. I don't know if you're engaged to that girl or something, but could we possibly meet in the cafeteria for a soda, perhaps some afternoon?" Elizabeth was surprised by her boldness. Fleetingly, she wondered if she had gone too far.

"I would like that. I appreciate the invitation. My only reservation is about Monica—that's the girl I've been dating. I don't want to upset her."

"I've thought about that, but it's not like you're engaged, is it?"

"Well, no, although she has talked about getting engaged."

There was silence for a few moments. Then Ryan, his countenance brightening, said, "I'm not beholden to her. There's no reason I shouldn't meet you next Tuesday in the cafeteria. Will after the two-p.m. class work for you?"

"Yes, that will be fine. I'm looking forward to getting to know you. That makes me one of a, ah, four-hundred other Stanton girls." She wasn't sure, but Elizabeth thought she saw a trace of blush cross Ryan's face.

Elizabeth was both excited and worried about her cafeteria date with Ryan. She anguished over what to wear, what to talk about, and—most importantly—how to ensure there would be future dates with Ryan. That prospect thrilled her, but also, she realized, it guaranteed a showdown with Monica.

The cafeteria was almost empty when Elizabeth arrived. Ryan appeared only a minute or two after her arrival. He seemed out of breath.

"I didn't want. . . to be late. I hope I didn't keep you. . . waiting."

"You didn't keep me waiting. I got here only a minute before you. How are you? You look wonderful."

"Thank you. You're too kind."

They ordered Cokes from a student who was working at the soda fountain. As they sat down at a booth, Elizabeth said, "You didn't answer my question. How have you been?"

"I've been hitting the books, haven't had much time for anything social—until now."

"For once, my timing was right," Elizabeth said.

They talked briefly about the election of student body officers last spring semester. Ryan was a junior and, against his will, had been nominated as one of ten candidates to serve as president for the 1936-37 school year, beginning with the fall semester. When the votes were counted, he emerged as student body president.

"You must be extra busy. . . ah, let's see, you're in office now and will serve until the end of the spring semester when a new president will take over—right?"

"That's right. I'm spending a lot of time in the SUB where I have my office. I wish Harold—he's a long-time friend—hadn't nominated me. But, Stanton has been good to me. I owe the school something." As an afterthought, Ryan added, "I'm sure you'll be approached by Harold. . .he thinks he has a monopoly on Stanton girls. Be prepared. He's a smooth operator."

Elizabeth appreciated the "by the way" information about Harold, but she was confident she could take care of herself. She had been on many dates in the future.

As they were leaving the cafeteria, Elizabeth resisted the urge to say something about a second date. "It's up to him," she told herself. "If he asks me, it will be a sign I'm giving Monica some competition."

Before they separated, Ryan couldn't resist giving Elizabeth a quick hug.

Touching her in some way, however innocent, was a desire he would give in to many times before their first kiss.

Later, on her way back to her apartment, Elizabeth saw Ryan and Monica in a line waiting to purchase tickets to the movie *Swing Time* with Fred Astaire and Ginger Rogers. Elizabeth hoped Ryan didn't see her, but he did.

"Hey, Elizabeth, come over here. There's someone I want you to meet."

It was the last thing Elizabeth wanted to do at that moment, but she complied.

"This is Monica," Ryan said, "she's a very good friend.

And Monica, this is Elizabeth, she's— "

"Actually, we're more than good friends—we're practically engaged," Monica broke in, a hint of irritation in her voice.

Ryan's face darkened momentarily.

"It's nice to meet you," Elizabeth said, looking directly at Monica. "I'm sure we'll meet again. Enjoy the movie—Fred Astaire and Ginger Rogers are among my favorites." She smiled to herself because she had seen that movie when she was eighteen on the Oldie-but-Goodie movie channel.

Elizabeth was puzzled why Ryan insisted on introducing her to Monica. What was his motive? Was it his way of telling Elizabeth that Monica was still his girlfriend? Or was he playing "hard to get?" Or— the complicated person he seemed to be—maybe he was just being friendly.

The next day, Elizabeth found an envelope under her door. "Elizabeth" was scribbled on it. She couldn't open it fast enough. A note inside read: *Dear Elizabeth, I know this is rushed—we've been only on one date—but please know I have been thinking about you, a lot. I haven't contacted you because Monica is intensely jealous of you. I want to see you again.*

I think you want that as well. But we must be careful. Meet me tonight at ten-thirty in the faculty parking lot and I will explain. Thank you. Ryan.

Elizabeth thought ten-thirty would never come. She attended her classes but paid little attention to the professors' lectures.

As she approached the faculty parking lot, she saw that Ryan was already there. He greeted Elizabeth with what struck her as a worried look. "I need to let you in on something, Elizabeth," he began, his voice tense. "Monica's father is in the state legislature; in fact, he's a senior senator. . . has a lot of influence. He likes me and wants me to marry Monica."

"Oh, I see."

"'He has hinted at helping me get a good position in state government. So, ah, I have to keep dating Monica. Do you understand the bind I'm in?"

"Yes, I get it. But at some point there has to be a resolution. I think the question you need to ask is 'What will make you happiest?' It's your life."

"You force me to confess what I've been holding back. I really like you, Elizabeth. You might as well know it. That's why this Monica thing is so difficult for me."

"You obviously don't prefer me enough to stand up to Monica's father, do you? For all I know, you <u>really</u> do like Monica better than me, and you've concocted a cover story."

"No, it's not that way at all," Ryan pleaded. "There is something about you, besides your incredible attractiveness, that makes me think you are from another time. I feel I have known you before. I know that sounds crazy, yet I cannot deny what I feel."

"What you feel is real. I <u>am</u> from another time."

"You <u>are</u>?"

"I lived decades from now. I was part of a conventional family, with a father, mother, and little brother. Unfortunately, my father was very controlling. Anyway, the world was filled with technology-driven wonders . . . television—like radio but with pictures—computers that revolutionized communication and research. . .pocket-sized telephones with which you could talk with someone thousands of miles away. . . doctors transplanting the heart . . . huge airplanes carrying hundreds of passengers across the Atlantic and Pacific oceans. . . manned rockets landing on the moon. Oh, Ryan, it was totally different."

"That's incredible, almost unbelievable. Thank you for telling me about it, gorgeous."

"I didn't mean to change the discussion. I understand your situation with Monica and her father. Please know I'll do everything I can, including dating other boys." As she spoke, Elizabeth's mind focused on Ryan's use of "gorgeous." "Clearly, he likes me," she thought to herself. "He's never called me that before." She giggled.

As if he were reading Elizabeth's mind, Ryan gave Elizabeth a peck on the cheek.

"I hope that was OK."

"It was fine, thank you," Elizabeth said, holding back a grin. "I hope there's more where that came from."

Ryan's face was smothered in a smile.

After a giggle-filled pause, they agreed that they must not be seen together.

"But how will we communicate?" Elizabeth asked.

Ryan thought a moment, then said, "Let's go back to exchanging notes, like grade-school kids."

"Where will we leave them?" Elizabeth asked, adding, "It's got to be an out-of-the-way place, of course."

"There's a crack around part of the cornerstone on the northeast corner of the original building," Ryan said. "We could deposit and pick up notes there."

"You must show me the exact spot—where the crack is."

"I'm going to walk you home. I'll take you there on the way."

En route, Ryan suddenly stopped in the shadow of a large oak tree. He turned, embraced Elizabeth, and kissed her—fully and firmly—on the lips. It was the first real kiss he had given her.

Elizabeth's toes curled.

The next day, Elizabeth passed Ryan between classes. She wanted to talk with him because she was still thinking of the previous night's kiss. But with unfortunate timing, Harold suddenly appeared. He said,

"Today is your lucky day. I'm free tomorrow. Do you want to go ice skating with me?"

Elizabeth readily accepted Harold's offer because she had been on several enjoyable dates with him after Ryan introduced them one night in the library. Ryan was confident he would end up winning Elizabeth's heart.

Moreover, he appreciated Harold's involvement because student government business was taking more and more of his time tying up loose ends as the ending of his first semester as president approached.

Elizabeth fell only twice at the rink. Harold helped her up each time, holding her more tightly than she thought necessary. Before leaving the rink, they stopped for a cup of hot cocoa and a donut. There was inevitably an awkward moment at her apartment door when it was time to say goodnight. Elizabeth always ended it by giving him a big hug. Each time, Harold wished for more because he liked Elizabeth.

Ryan's note-exchanging plan was a failure. Harold, who had been spying on Elizabeth, caught her putting a note by the cornerstone.

Harold went as soon as possible to Lester Williams and told him Ryan and Elizabeth were in contact with each other, and that Ryan preferred Elizabeth to Monica.

Lester's face turned pepper red. He gave the news to Monica, who went furious. Then he dictated the following letter to Ryan and had his secretary deliver it. It read:

> *Ryan, you will recall that I promised to get you an important job in state government if you continued to court Monica and when the time was right marry her. Monica and I have learned, through the student grapevine, that you are being deceitful. You are forsaking her for Elizabeth. My offer is off the table. Yours truly, Lester.*

Later, Monica shouted at Ryan as he was leaving the bookstore.

"What a poor excuse you are for a man! You and your cheap blonde girlfriend are nothing but tramps. I never want to see you again."

Ryan shrugged off Monica's comments. He had seen similar behavior from her before. He was actually pleased with the Williams letter and Monica's outburst.

"Do you know what that means?" Ryan asked Elizabeth.

Answering his question, he said, "It means we don't have to hide our love from anyone anymore, and we are free of the burdens our relationship with Lester and Monica placed on us. I couldn't be happier."

"You gave up an important position at the state level for me," Elizabeth said soberly. Then, voice breaking, she added, "You really do love me. You really do. Thank you, my beautiful man."

Ryan went to the ticket office in the Administration Building where he purchased two tickets for the Snowball Dance.

5

Challenge

Ryan didn't look like a black-belted kind of man. He was soft-spoken, mild-mannered, kind, and polite. Elizabeth saw another side of him, however, one night at Stanton's gym.

Ryan and Elizabeth were jogging around the University's oval-shaped indoor track. The track had resilient flooring, which made it especially suitable for joggers with knee problems. Five non-students were at one end of the track. As Ryan and Elizabeth approached that end, the non-students began to throw volleyballs at them. At first, they threw with a light force, but then they began to throw harder each time the pair got near them. One of the high-velocity balls, which had been kicked, hit Elizabeth in the face, causing a nosebleed, considerable pain, and temporary blindness.

After escorting Elizabeth to a seat on the sidelines and getting her a towel, Ryan went to the group, "Who kicked the ball that hit my girlfriend?" he asked. One especially well-built youth raised his hand. Ryan approached him. As he did so, "Rocky," as he was known, struck a blow to Ryan's face, followed by a kick to his groin. Ryan grabbed Rocky by the collar, started to twist it, and said, "Listen, pal, do you really want to take me on?" Then Ryan gave the collar a full twist, driving Rocky to the floor.

One of Rocky's companions, seeing that he wasn't getting up, and sensing he needed to show loyalty, took several wild swings at Ryan. One landed on Ryan's throat, causing him to gasp for breath. He recovered in time to block a second blow to his throat and to deliver a crushing, fight-ending uppercut. Ryan's hand would hurt for days.

A Stanton security officer appeared. He was making evening rounds.

Elizabeth, traumatized by having witnessed the incident, haltingly told the officer what had happened—how it started and what ensued.

She was pleased to see he was taking notes.

The officer got the names of the perpetrators by checking the identification they had with them. While Ryan was tending to his hand, the officer said to Rocky and those with him, "Be prepared for repercussions. The administration will contact you. Now, get out of here!"

Elizabeth and Ryan wondered if "unfriendly friends" had instigated the attack, but dismissed that idea.

From that night forward, though she suspected as much, Elizabeth knew that in Ryan she had a man with the will and the strength to protect her in virtually any circumstance. She told Ryan as much. She knew something else, as well: Her decision to stay in the past with Ryan was right. That knowledge was conveniently confirmed when she heard Ryan say:

"No one threatens you or hurts you and goes free. I abhor violence directed at anyone, but if it's directed at someone dear to me, I will do whatever is necessary. Maybe that sounds like boasting, but it's the truth."

Ryan couldn't remember having received a tighter hug.

6

Suitors

Ryan knew that many Stanton young men approached Elizabeth for dates. He didn't lose sleep over that. He told Elizabeth, "I want you to date other men. You should have an opportunity to compare them to me." Not long after the ice-skating date with Harold, Stanton's star basketball player caught up with Elizabeth in the cafeteria.

"Hi, Liz," he said, "you may know me, or at least know who I am."

"Oh, um, I think you're an athlete. Must be basketball, you're so tall. That's it, you're on Stanton's basketball team."

"I'm flattered that you recognized me. My name's Jim, Jim Murphy. I play center on the team."

"Center—that figures. It's nice to meet you, Jim. How is the team doing? In what place—"

"Oh, fairly well," Jim said dismissively, eager to move the conversation. "Listen, Liz, I'd like to take you out. Would you be willing to go out with me, say to a movie, or maybe just to dinner? I've been longing for an opportunity to approach you. Guys notice you."

"A date sounds nice. By the way, I don't go by 'Liz,'—it's 'Elizabeth'— just so you know."

"Oh, sorry."

After two or three minutes of discussion, they set a date. Jim said he would pick her up at six for dinner at one of the town's premier restaurants. "He is good-looking and sort of charming," she said to herself as they parted.

Elizabeth would remember her date with Jim for a long time: it was a disaster, except that the food was excellent. The only thing Jim talked about was basketball. Later, in describing the date to Ryan, she told him that Jim was the most self-centered person she had ever met. "I think he thinks he's the center of the universe, not just on a basketball court," she told Ryan.

"And it wasn't just all his basketball talk."

"You mean he tried to get physical with you? Some athletes are infamous for that sort of thing."

"That's an understatement with him. I think he thought I was a slam dunk."

Despite her bad experience with Jim, Elizabeth, heeding Ryan's counsel, accepted more dates with Stanton men.

One was with red-headed John, who was majoring in philosophy. In a booth in a restaurant, he confirmed his reputation for being an off-putting intellectual.

"Why, Elizabeth, is there something? Wouldn't it be easier if there were nothing?"

"Frankly, I haven't thought of that."

"Well, it's a classic philosophical question. I'm surprised you haven't addressed it."

John asked Elizabeth similar questions, and expressed alarm about her answers.

The date ended early, and mercifully, as they were leaving the restaurant.

"Thanks for going out with me. I've got to leave to attend a Friends of Philosophy meeting. See ya."

Elizabeth found her way home.

Another forgettable date was with George, a full-of-himself, non-stop talker. He had invited Elizabeth to accompany him to an exhibit of the magazine covers created by Norman Rockwell. The exhibit was in the University's library. George insisted on driving Elizabeth to the library even though it was only a short walk away. Elizabeth surmised he was eager to show off his new car, a 1936 Morgan 4/4. She made the mistake of asking George to tell her about himself. They were still in the car an hour later. George was still talking, and Elizabeth was sound asleep. As he pulled up to her apartment, and she awakened, she said, "You know, George, I've had many nice evenings, but this wasn't one of them. Good night."

7

Storm

Ryan decided to take Elizabeth on a picnic after class, even though afternoons were beginning to get cool. Ryan knew a spot in the foothills east of the campus. It was two-p.m. when they started for the site.

Elizabeth had prepared a light lunch, and they both had jackets.

As they were leaving, Walt Stevens, a farmer in his late thirties who owned land next to the University, saw them and wished them a happy outing. They thanked him.

"Nice guy," Ryan said to Elizabeth.

Ryan had been wanting to ask Elizabeth if she had any idea who was sponsoring her and who was paying all her expenses. He posed the question while they were hiking. "I wish I knew. I would like to thank them. But the fact is, I don't know." Uncomfortable with the question, Elizabeth changed the subject. "How far is this place?"

"We can be there by three, eat our lunch, and be back by five," Ryan said. He added, "It doesn't get dark until six or so."

There was a well-worn trail to the site, but Ryan took what he called a "secret trail." "It's a lot more interesting and there's more to see," he told Elizabeth. "We will have to cross a bridge, though, and it's rickety."

"Hmm, sounds like a male thing. Well, you know I trust you completely."

After they had been on the "secret trail" for a few minutes, Elizabeth concluded that it wasn't a secret at all. Almost everybody knew about it, but they avoided it because of the bridge. That was her hunch, which she confirmed as soon as she saw the bridge. Boards were missing, and the middle section was partly underwater.

Ryan saw apprehension in Elizabeth's eyes and sought to reassure her. "It isn't as bad as it looks. I'll be holding your hand all the way."

"Uh-huh, that way we'll sink to the bottom together, right?"

The river wasn't deep, but the prospect of falling into the fast-moving water terrified Elizabeth. The thought occurred to her that maybe Ryan was testing her trust in him.

Almost halfway across, Ryan decided they should turn back.

"It just isn't worth the risk. Besides, the weather is turning bad. A storm is brewing."

A huge thunderclap sounded just as they got off the bridge. Heavy rainfall and wicked winds followed. Ryan grabbed Elizabeth's arm. There was urgency in his grip.

"I know of an old cabin," he said, and with Elizabeth at his side, they raced to it.

Although the roof leaked, the cabin provided some protection from the storm, which seemed to get stronger.

Ryan found a large piece of plywood and wedged it between the roof joists They sat on the floor beneath it, and Elizabeth retrieved the sandwiches she had prepared.

"It looks like we're going to have to spend the night here," Ryan said. "It's raining harder than ever."

Ryan realized his comment could have depressed Elizabeth, so he changed the subject. He asked a question somewhat similar to the one he had asked when they were hiking. He wanted to get her mind off their present circumstances, but he also wanted an answer.

"I'm wondering if you've thought about the quality of life you will be giving up if you stay here—in 1936—with me. As you have told me, the time period you left offers benefits, comforts, and advantages far superior to what you will have here. Don't misunderstand, I want you here, desperately so, but have you considered what you will be giving up?"

"Of course, I've thought about it. I don't want a life without you. I can't make it any clearer than that. Understand?"

"Yes. Thank you. I won't bring it up again."

'There's something else I want you to understand, Ryan. I have said little about it. I was afraid you might find it offputting, but I need to be forthright about it, and now's a good time. It goes like the following. Because my father was extremely controlling, he wouldn't let my mother leave the house without his permission. I became interested in the women's rights movement. In my sophomore year of college, I organized a society devoted to helping coeds understand the degree to which women are treated as second-class citizens in America. I told them about the work of Susan Anthony. I think they received valuable insight. Based on that experience, I intend to approach Stanton's governing board about creating a women's rights department. Are you OK with that?"

"I think that's a stellar idea, Elizabeth. I have long wondered, for example, why women are paid substantially less than men for doing the same work. I think you should go for it, but not until we're married. Our plans for marriage should have the priority right now."

"I agree."

"By the way, regarding this experience we're having, I know someone who, when he hears about us in this cabin, will be all too happy," Elizabeth said. "He'll make it sound sordid . . . like we spent the night here so we could have sex," Elizabeth said. She added, "He will use it to break us up and have himself take your place."

"Perhaps so, but I don't think that will work," Ryan said, as he wrapped his arms around his shivering companion to keep her warm.

Both listened intently for a letup in the rain. "Even if it stopped, could we find our way out?" Elizabeth asked, a touch of anger in her voice.

"You have every right to be mad at me," Ryan responded, hugging her even more firmly.

Elizabeth didn't answer.

Despite the cold, or perhaps because of it, they fell asleep in each other's arms.

8

Friend

Walt Stevens wasn't falling to sleep. The rain rattled his bedroom window, which took his thoughts to his brief encounter with Ryan and Elizabeth. Suddenly, he wondered if they might be trapped in the forest. A sense of urgency overtook him. He fairly jumped out of bed, put on his winter clothes, grabbed a flashlight, and headed for the trail that led into the forest.

The forest ground seemed like a swamp. Each footstep sank inches into the ground.

Walt didn't know the route they took, so he made a guess and began calling Ryan's name. He received no response, but he knew about the cabin and headed for it, calling Ryan's name as he did so.

"Listen, listen. Someone's calling your name," Elizabeth said between shivers. Ryan rushed out the door and answered, "We're here. . . here at the old cabin!"

In only minutes, Walt was at the cabin, and Elizabeth was crying tears of joy.

"How did . . . how did you know we were here?" Elizabeth asked, through chattering teeth.

Before Walt could answer, Ryan reminded Elizabeth that they had met Walt on their way into the forest. Then he said, "Walt knows how unforgiving a major storm can be. He's a farmer, has been for probably twenty years. He knows the land and how life-threatening it can be.

He knew we had gone into the forest and wondered if we had gotten out before the storm hit. He worried about us and couldn't sleep. Is that how it happened, Walt?"

"Yes, that's about it," Walt replied.

Walt escorted them out of the forest to his house, where they got out of their wet clothes, dried themselves with a bundle of towels, and put on clothes Walt provided.

When they were warm and dry, Walt drove them to their apartments in his battered farm truck.

By mutual agreement, Ryan and Elizabeth didn't go to school the next day because they had missed a whole night's sleep. They stayed in their apartments and slept most of the day. The forest experience gave them insight into how fortunate they were to have warm, dry, safe places to stay.

Harold went to school that morning as usual. En route, he stopped his roadster at one of Logandale's two gas stations. As he was waiting for the attendant, Walt Stevens arrived at the station in his old truck. Harold knew Walt because he had taken one of Walt's daughters to Stanton High's junior prom.

"Hey, Walt, how are you? I see you're still driving that wreck. What's new, anyway?"

"Nothing wrong with this truck, Harold. It will outlast that toy you call a car . . . will outlast it for years. As for what's new, I had an interesting experience last night—or I should say early this morning."

"At your age, I can't imagine that it was very interesting," Harold said, laughing.

"Remember last night's terrible storm?"

Harold nodded.

"Well, Ryan and Elizabeth got caught in the forest in the middle of it. I had seen them go into the forest in the afternoon, and later, when I was in bed, I wondered if they got out. I got up, quickly dressed. . . found them in that old cabin."

With raised eyebrows, Harold said, "How interesting after all. . . fascinating in fact." Harold, seeing one last chance to replace Ryan as Elizabeth's preferred man, then thanked Walt profusely.

Harold and Ed Skanky, the overweight editor of the *Stanton Sentinel,* were old friends. Harold wasted no time in trying to capitalize on that friendship. He went to Skanky's office right after his first class.

"Did you know that Ryan and Elizabeth spent last night in that old cabin—just the two of them?" he asked Skanky, his voice brimming with drama.

"Are you suggesting that Ryan and Elizabeth had sex that night?" the blunt-talking Skanky asked Harold.

"I don't know that for a fact, but it's certainly not unreasonable to assume they did. I mean, a, ah, they were alone in a cabin. They're crazy about each other. Do you think they spent the night playing Chinese Checkers? I think 'it' happened, and most of your readers will think the same thing."

"What am I to say in the article about the source? Who claims to know about what happened in the cabin? I have to cite a source or a witness."

"Can't you just say an 'unidentified source' gave you the information—a source that asked not to be named?"

"Look, Harold, "I'm not going to play games with my readers, which is what you're asking me to do. If you can't provide credible evidence for your story, I want no part of it."

"And I thought we were friends!" Harold fairly screamed at Skanky.

"Well, that friendship is over," he said as he stomped out the door.

Harold didn't give up easily. Skanky's refusal to do his bidding made Harold even more determined to damage Ryan's reputation which would cause Elizabeth to turn her attention to him, so he hoped. After all, Harold reasoned, it was Ryan's idea to take Elizabeth into the forest late in the afternoon. Was it just a picnic he had in mind?

With the aid of his friends, Harold began a word-of-mouth

campaign. According to Harold, Ryan took Elizabeth into the forest and planned to use the cabin for illicit purposes. He had no knowledge of the approaching storm.

Most students who heard Harold's campaign story didn't believe it. They had too much respect for Ryan and Elizabeth. Moreover, some believed there was a competition between Harold and Ryan for Elizabeth's hand.

Harold's campaign failed miserably. Ryan made sure it was dead by getting Skanky to publish a letter to the editor, worded:

Dear Students,

Perhaps you have heard the rumor that I spent the night with Elizabeth in the old cabin in the foothills east of campus. I <u>was</u> in the cabin with Elizabeth. We sought shelter there when the terrible storm ended our plans to have a picnic. The suggestion that something immoral happened there is utterly false. Someone has made Elizabeth and myself the victims of a vicious rumor. I know you will dismiss the rumor for what it is—slander. Thank you.

The rumors stopped. Harold realized he couldn't compete with Ryan for Elizabeth's heart. Consequently, he courted Monica. He did so for more than a week, before approaching Lester Williams, Monica's father.

"I'm aware, sir, of the agreement you had with Ryan."

"It's true. I told Ryan I would help him get an important job in state government if he married Monica. Is it that to which you refer?"

"Yes, it is, and I—"

"Let me make it easy for you, Harold. Monica has told me you are courting her, having accepted the fact that Elizabeth and Ryan are a done deal. Now you want to know that if you marry Monica will I transfer the agreement I had with Ryan to you. In other words, would

I get you a significant position in state government. I must say, that request is gutsy of you."

"Yes, I realize that."

"I admire your gumption. It's time Monica accepted what might be called Plan B—namely you. So, yes, you have a deal."

"Thank you, sir. Thank you."

They shake hands.

9

Conflict

Despite their love for one another, Elizabeth and Ryan sometimes argued. Elizabeth felt that, under the circumstances, that was to be expected.

"I think our arguments, though minor, are grounded in the fact I grew up in an environment totally foreign to you," she told Ryan.

"I've thought about that," Ryan said. "I think it raises the question about nature versus nurture. In our case, it's clearly nurture."

"Yes, and the nurturing you received has affected your angle of vision—I like that term—that is, the way you see and analyze things. And of course, the same is true for me."

"I think of that silly argument we had about fried food," Ryan said. "I objected to your fondness for fried food. I think I said something to the effect that it was unhealthy, which put you on the defensive."

"I didn't think of it, but I should have pointed out that where I come from fried food is extremely popular and readily available at fast-food places located all over the city. My parents took me and my brother to those places probably once or twice a week, especially hamburger joints that came with French fries. I loved that. My brother and I looked upon it as a form of parental love or as a reward."

"I never had that, not from my parents and not from my aunt and uncle," Ryan said. "So, I had difficulty understanding your fondness for fried food, and—as a result—we argued about it."

"That validates the wisdom of the counsel when you have a difference with someone, seek first to understand where they're coming from before stating your position. If you do that, you may well change your position."

Elizabeth added that it's important to know the background of the person you're dealing with. She told Ryan she knew, from friends, that a drunk driver had killed his parents when he was seven, and that his aunt and uncle raised him. When he turned eighteen, he received his parents' large estate, and he had been on his own since then.

"Thank you. I knew I wasn't a complete mystery to you," Ryan said.

"There's another factor, a big one, that accounts for how we see things differently. It's gender. Men's and women's brains are different. Men, as you know, tend to be more dominant and assertive. That's why, for centuries, they have kept many rights to themselves, a condition that exists today in many places, and it's why I am an advocate for women's rights. I know I've mentioned this to you before, but not in the same way."

Ryan nodded in agreement.

"What I'm about to say isn't directly related to what you just said, but I want to toss it in because it deals with human relationships," Ryan said.

"I think we're getting too serious," Elizabeth said, "but go ahead."

"Well, two weeks ago or so, a visiting English professor was lecturing about the parts of speech—nouns, pronouns, adjectives, and so on. She asked the class, 'What do you think are the most important pronouns in terms of human relationships?' Sean, a very sharp student, raised his hand and said "I" and "you."

"Right on!" the professor said.

"That makes sense to me," Elizabeth said. So, let me remind you, Ryan, that **I** love **you**."

They both laughed.

For lunch, Ryan took Elizabeth to one of the few eateries in Logandale that served hamburgers.

10

Founders

The semester was nearing an end, and as it did so, virtually everyone at Stanton was looking forward to two events: The Founders' Day Banquet and the Snowball Dance. Ryan had made sure weeks earlier that he and Elizabeth had dates for those events.

"The administration goes all-out to make those events extra special," Ryan told Elizabeth.

"I'm sure they're very nice, but before we can enjoy them, we have to take end-of-semester exams," Elizabeth said. "As smart as you are, that probably isn't a big concern, but it's a huge concern for me."

"You'll ace those exams, Sweetie. You have got nothing to worry about."

Ryan didn't tell Elizabeth that as student body president, he would be one of the Founders' Day Banquet speakers. He wanted to surprise her.

The event lived up to its billing. The University auditorium was lavishly decorated. Guests were seated at round tables where a no-expense-spared dinner was served. The governor was the featured speaker. His remarks, dynamic and riveting, resulted in a standing ovation. He warned his audience about "troubling developments" in Europe and said a horrific war was "not out of the question." He was followed by three Stanton graduates, going back several years, who had been highly successful. Each attributed much of their success to their Stanton education.

As dessert was being served, Ryan stepped to the podium as the concluding speaker.

He thanked everyone for their support, noting that whatever he had accomplished in his "inaugural semester" resulted from that support.

Then, inspired by what Elizabeth had said about the future, he told his audience they would live to see the "impossible become possible." "We will live in an age that events once considered miracles will become commonplace. Be prepared for far-reaching changes in your lives. Radio is great, but it's nothing compared to what is to come."

Then he said, "Some have wondered why Mr. Stanton built this university in an out-of-the-way place. He could have built it where it would attract a lot of attention and given him rewarding publicity and acclaim. But he chose Logandale. Yes, he liked its peaceful, quiet setting. But there was more to it than that. In the library's archives, I found a letter he wrote to a faculty member who was teaching atheism. Here is an excerpt:"

> *There is living evidence of divine design just outside your window. Who with eyes to see can miss the message? Think of patterns. When did you last look at the veins of a leaf, or an etching of algae framed by granite? Think of symmetry. The perfectly matched markings on a pair of butterfly wings... the marshaled precision of sunflower petals. Who with ears to hear can miss the music? Think of the harmony of wind and water at a canyon campsite at nightfall, There, in the clear mountain air, looking at the underside of an umbrella of stars, one knows that this is matter organized and that it cannot be the result of some kind of cosmic lottery.*

Ladies and Genlemen. We have every reason to be proud of our heritage—to honor it and hold it sacred. Mr. Stanton was more than a businessman and philanthropist. He was a man of faith who revered life in all its forms and who sought to protect it and nourish it. That includes your life and mine, and the lives of all who will follow us at this, our cherished university."

Thank you, and goodnight.

Ryan's twenty-minute speech received almost as much applause as the governor's.

When the banquet ended, Ryan was greeted with handshakes and hugs accompanied by expressions of praise and congratulation. Elizabeth looked on, eyes glistening.

The auditorium's lights were dimming as Ryan began walking Elizabeth back to her dorm room. En route, he squeezed her hand even more tightly and stopped at an ornate, wrought-iron bench by a lamp post.

"I have written something for you," he said, as they sat down. He withdrew a paper from his suit jacket.

"It's a poem. Oh, Sweetheart, I so hope you like it."

"I know I will, incredible man."

Ryan, angling the paper to take advantage of the lamp's light, read the poem, voice enveloped in emotion.

> *Love, take my hand, trust my heart*
> *be mine in timeless tomorrows.*
> *God's own daughter thou truly art*
> *fearless, faithful in joy and sorrows.*
>
> *Embrace my life, make us one*
> *be at my side at every turn.*

Hold me close when day is done
and show me what I've yet to learn.

Know that you and I were meant to be
'tis a truth every angel could foresee.
Love, take my hand, never leave
trust my heart . . . and believe.

Elizabeth sobbed softly in gratitude and joy. She moved onto Ryan's lap, pressed the palms of her hands against the sides of his face, and gave him a kiss that would live with him forever.

11

Disclosure

With the 1936 Founders' Day Banquet "history" and exams completed, Ryan turned his attention to the last social event of the semester, the Stanton Snowball Dance.

"You know, Sweetheart, you haven't yet formally asked me to marry you, have you?"

"Well, ah, no, I haven't."

"A woman deserves to receive an official proposal—right, big guy?"

Elizabeth had seldom seen Ryan blush, but he did so then. He was quiet for a moment and then said, "I've been holding off because I want to propose just before the dance. That way everybody will know about it, and it will be dramatic… really dramatic."

"Hmmm…that *will* be dramatic. Great idea!" Suddenly, though, Elizabeth looked very serious.

"What's wrong?" Ryan asked, reading her countenance.

You deserve to know, at least as much as I know. You asked about my benefactor, and I wasn't able to give you an answer. The truth is, I still don't know."

"How can you <u>still</u> not know? Ryan sounded irritated.

"I can shed a little light.

I had attended a community college in my hometown. I did well academically and got a scholarship to Stanton. So, I left my family and traveled to Logandale. I stayed in an apartment rented to me by Mrs.

Ravencroft. At Mrs. Ravencroft's I found a yearbook titled *The Year That Was: Stanton University, 1937.* In it, I found your picture. I was completely 'taken' by it. I became obsessed with you. I had to find a way to meet you, as silly as that sounds."

Elizabeth tells Ryan that Mrs. Ravencroft's mother attended Stanton at the same time as him. "According to Mrs. Ravencroft, her mother said you, Ryan, was a student body officer and that your office was in the SUB. I went to the building. Incredibly, I found your desk, and—even more incredibly—I found an envelope with my name written on it. Inside were two tickets to the Stanton Snowball Dance. They had been torn in half but taped back together. As I held the tickets, a warm feeling came over me. I felt I was floating. The next thing I knew, I was on the Stanton campus in 1936—here, with you."

"That account leaves me breathless," Ryan said. "It also leaves me worried. What if you go back to the future and I lose you?"

"I can't bear to think about that, so I won't try to answer. Hmmm, let's see, I think you asked me a question before I told you about how I got here. The answer is, Yes, darling man, I will marry you. Yes, yes, yes!"

The next day Elizabeth and Ryan went shopping for an engagement ring. Elizabeth chose a silver ring with a "round brilliant" diamond. She couldn't wear it right away because it had to be sized. That pleased Ryan because he wanted to propose and give Elizabeth the ring just before the dance.

Elizabeth and Ryan went to the jeweler's the next day to get the ring. The jeweler handed it to Ryan and deadpanned, "I think you know what to do with this." Ryan took Elizabeth by the left hand and said, "You'll excuse us for a moment," whereupon he gave Elizabeth a long, passionate kiss.

Ryan had a gift for always saying the right thing. He looked at the ring in silence for a full two minutes. Elizabeth worried that something was wrong, as did the jeweler. Then Ryan said, "The ring is beautiful in and by itself, but on your finger, it is beyond beautiful. Maybe that's because of what it means—what it symbolizes—rather than just what it looks like."

"I think that's a profound statement," Elizabeth said. "Thank you, Sweetheart."

Ryan then directed Elizabeth's attention to their relationship with Harold.

"We need to repair our relationship with him. I don't want it to end with us as enemies."

"Neither do I," Elizabeth said.

"I suggest we invite Harold to meet with us in my office. The sooner the better, say tomorrow at ten. We can apologize for any wrongs—real or imagined—we may have committed against him and tell him we want to be friends again. What do you think?"

"I like that. It's the civil thing to do."

Harold arrived at Ryan's office the next day, a few minutes before ten.

As soon as he saw Harold's face, Ryan knew reconciliation would not be easy. "Harold virtually never loses when differences surface in human relationships," Ryan told Elizabeth. "Invariably, he gets his way. Now, however, he is losing."

Ryan tried to break the ice by suggesting Harold and Monica double date to the dance with him and Elizabeth. He reached into his desk drawer, held up the tickets, and said, "I already have tickets, and more are available at the ticket—"

With blinding quickness, Harold swiped the tickets from Ryan's hand and tore them in half.

Elizabeth was horrified as she felt herself drifting away and returning to the present. In the distance, she heard Ryan frantically calling her name, over and over, until she could no longer hear him.

The feeling of moving through space abruptly ended when she saw she was in the soon-to-be-demolished SUB. She was beyond being devastated. She went to her apartment. As she approached,

Mrs. Ravencroft, who had been looking out the window, saw her and confronted her.

"Where have you been?"

Mrs. Ravencroft knew the answer, but she wanted confirmation from Elizabeth.

Afraid that Mrs. Ravencroft would criticize her answer or make light of it, Elizabeth didn't answer but went directly to her room.

"No, no, no!" Ryan screamed as he saw Elizabeth disappear. "It's just what I feared. She's gone ahead—to the future. I may never see her again! I can't stand that thought."

Harold was dumbfounded, but said to Ryan, "Looks like you can't have her either," his voice radiating satisfaction.

Ryan taped the torn tickets back together, inserted them into an envelope on which he wrote "Elizabeth," and taped it to the desk drawer.

In her room, Elizabeth was sobbing uncontrollably.

She could not sleep, tossing and turning the night away. At dawn's light, she dressed quickly, almost frantically, repeatedly telling herself, "I must find a way back… I must, I must." She looked in the mirror and was shocked at what she saw; swollen eyes and tangled hair, but she didn't care. She tried to be quiet to avoid awakening Mrs. Ravencroft, but as she opened the door to leave, her eyes squarely met her landlady's. "I want you to have something," Mrs. Ravencroft said. I'm confident you'll make it back to 1936. When you do, and only then, read this letter." She handed Elizabeth an envelope and said "I will miss you," followed by a hug. Elizabeth emotionally echoed Mrs. Ravencroft's words, then turned quickly and headed for the SUB.

Fortunately, the door was unlocked, and all the debris was still scattered across the floor. She didn't know it then, but a strike by the Carpenter's Union had stopped the demolition of the building.

Otherwise, everything would have been gone.

She resolved to examine every square foot of the concrete floor and to do so on her hands and knees. She would look for *anything*, even a tiny scrap, that would tie her to Ryan and possibly take her back to him. It was exhausting work. Her arms ached, and she encountered rat droppings, ants, dust balls, and an assortment of trash. She was frantic and almost lost hope. As she approached the area where Ryan's desk was, she intensified her effort. The desk was in pieces. Someone had looted the top. Parts of the drawers were in a pile. She shuffled through them. And then, miraculously and unbelievably, she saw a large section of a drawer. An envelope labeled "Elizabeth" was taped on it. She dislodged the envelope and retrieved the two taped tickets. She held them over her heart.

Suddenly, she felt a hand on her shoulder. It was gentle, comforting, healing. She was being lifted up. Ryan was there, smiling.

He said, "Let's go home, Sweetheart."

12

Letter

Elizabeth was excited to read the letter Mrs. Ravencroft had given her. Ryan was excited as well. They sat down together. Elizabeth's hands were shaking as she opened the envelope, unfolded the letter, and read aloud the following.

> *Dear Elizabeth,*
>
> *If you're reading this, you successfully made it back to 1936. Congratulations!*
>
> *You deserve to know who your benefactor has been. There exists a society that operates in secret; hence it is known as the "Secret Society." All of its members are or were wealthy, including, of course, its founder. . . I do not know his name, but he was a former leader in the equal-rights-for-women movement. He knew Susan Anthony. He felt strongly that more women—many more—should be in leadership positions at all levels of government. He felt the place to start was to provide educational opportunities for young women of promise at Stanton University (his alma mater). He authored a new bylaw for the Society which states:*

"Members shall identify female high school and junior college graduates who have excelled academically and are of exemplary character. Full-ride scholarships to Stanton University shall be granted to fifteen such young women annually."

A representative from the society contacted your parents and told them that you were one of the fifteen chosen. He subsequently contacted me and asked me to assist you with housing and "whatever needs she may have." The representative who revealed most of the foregoing to me offered to give me $5,000 for my services. I declined, explaining that I needed something worthwhile to do.

The society had no way of knowing you would fall in love with a man decades younger than you. I find it fitting that you will be in a position to nurture the women's rights movement during the challenging 1930s.

I will be forever grateful for the blessing of knowing you.

With love and every good wish,

Mrs. Ravencroft

"Now we know, don't we, Sweetie?"

"Indeed," Ryan said. "I promise to not ask you questions for, ah, until my hair falls out."

13

Proposal

Elizabeth and Ryan arrived back in 1936 immediately, giving them ample time to get ready for the Snowball Dance, which would start at 8-p.m. They also had time for some innocent love-making. Ryan broke away and drove Elizabeth to her Scranton Dorm so she could dress for the dance. Then he drove to his apartment for the same purpose. By 7:30 he was back at her apartment. She looked more beautiful than he had ever seen her. He felt as if he were in heaven. They kissed. Quickly he was on his knees. Moments passed and then he spoke.

Dearest Elizabeth, my precious sweetheart, the light of my life, I love you with all of my heart. I want you more than anything in this world to be my wife. Will you marry me?

There were tears in Elizabeth's eyes as she answered "Yes." Ryan rose, took the ring from his pocket and slipped it onto her finger. They kissed and embraced, and did so again and again.

"Oh, darling, we're going to be late for the dance," Elizabeth said.

"Somehow, that doesn't seem important—" His lips are on hers again.

"Ryan!"

"You're right, Sweetheart. Let's go to the dance."

They enter the dance hall. It was beautifully decorated, but nothing was as beautiful to Elizabeth as the ring on her finger and the man in her arms.

14

Epilogue

During that evening when Elizabeth left with Ryan, Mrs. Ravencroft went to Room 2B. She looked for a few moments at the empty room. "I'm glad I played a part," she said aloud in her high-pitched voice.

"I know Elizabeth and Ryan will be happy and that Monica and Harold will be as well. Then she sighed the kind of sigh only the old appreciate and returned to her apartment. She went to a cupboard, opened its framed glass door, and withdrew a bulging, tattered scrapbook that her mother, Monica, had prepared. She laid it on a table and began turning the pages. She stopped at a page that displayed a newspaper clipping with the headline, Olsen Appointed State Supreme Court Aide. A caption for an accompanying photo read: *Harold C. Olsen is shown here with his wife Monica and seven-year-old daughter Bella. Olsen had just been sworn in as executive assistant to the court. He thanked retired Senator Lester Williams for his support.* She turned more pages and stopped at a clipping headlined Women's Rights Council Names Richardson President.

She smiled her crooked smile, closed the book, returned it to its place in the cupboard, and turned out the light.